ALAN'S BIG, SCARY TEETH

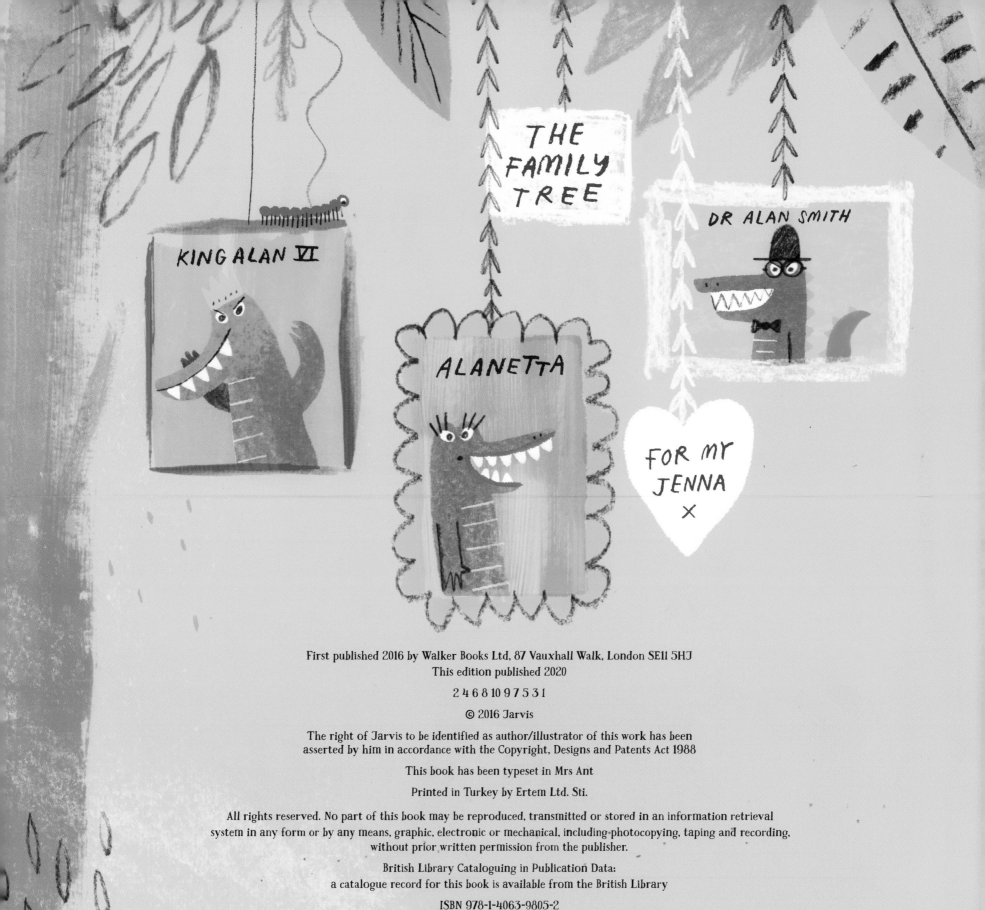

THE FAMILY TREE

KING ALAN VI

ALANETTA

DR ALAN SMITH

FOR MY JENNA x

First published 2016 by Walker Books Ltd, 87 Vauxhall Walk, London SE11 5HJ
This edition published 2020

2 4 6 8 10 9 7 5 3 1

© 2016 Jarvis

This book has been typeset in Mrs Ant

Printed in Turkey by Ertem Ltd. Sti.

British Library Cataloguing in Publication Data:
a catalogue record for this book is available from the British Library

ISBN 978-1-4063-9805-2

www.walker.co.uk

ALAN'S BIG, SCARY TEETH

by
JARVIS

WALKER BOOKS
AND SUBSIDIARIES
LONDON • BOSTON • SYDNEY • AUCKLAND

Alan came from a long line
of very scary alligators.
He was known throughout
the jungle for his scaring.

It was what he did best.

Alan would start each day ...

polishing his scales,
sharpening his nails ...

and brushing each of his
big, scary teeth for
(at least) ten minutes
at a time.

And after practising his frightening faces in the mirror ...

GRRR!

SNAP SNAP TOOTHPASTE

SHINY SHINY POLISH

EAU DE GATOR

he'd sneak into the jungle for his morning round of scaring.

WELCOME TO THE JUNGLE

Alan went, "SNAP! SNAP!"

SNAP! SNAP!

And, "GRRR! GRRR!"

GRRR! GRRR!

He said things like, "I'M BIG, SCARY ALAN! FEAR MY RAZOR-SHARP TEETH!"

He made the frogs leap off their lily pads, the monkeys tumble from the trees and the parrots screech in terrible terror.

SNAP! SNAP!

GRRR!

After a long day of scaring the jungle animals, Alan would head back home to the swamp, relax, finish the crossword in the *Jungle Times* and ...

TAKE OUT HIS FALSE TEETH!

NOBODY knew about
Alan's false teeth.

"Good night teeth. Thweet dweams my thcary thnappers," Alan would say, as he put them away carefully in his super-secret hiding place.

One morning, Barry the beaver was up early collecting wood and came across a dozing Alan.

Terrified that Alan might wake up and gobble him whole, he quickly dived behind a bush.

SNORT!
SNORT!

Phew! That was close, thought Barry, just as a set of false teeth fell out of a bush with a very familiar *"SNAP! SNAP!"*

When Alan awoke his teeth were GONE.
"MY TEETH! MY TEETH! WHERE ARE MY TEETH!"
What could he do?

Maybe no one would notice?

Could he still be scary without them? He decided to head into the jungle as usual.

He made the frogs
leap off their lily pads,
the monkeys tumble
from the trees and
the parrots screech ...

WITH LAUGHTER!

Alan just wasn't very scary
without his teeth.

Alan slunk back to the swamp. He had never been more embarrassed.

He came from a long line of very scary alligators. Scaring was all he had ever known.

What would Alan do now?

Poor Alan began to cry.
Just a bit at first...

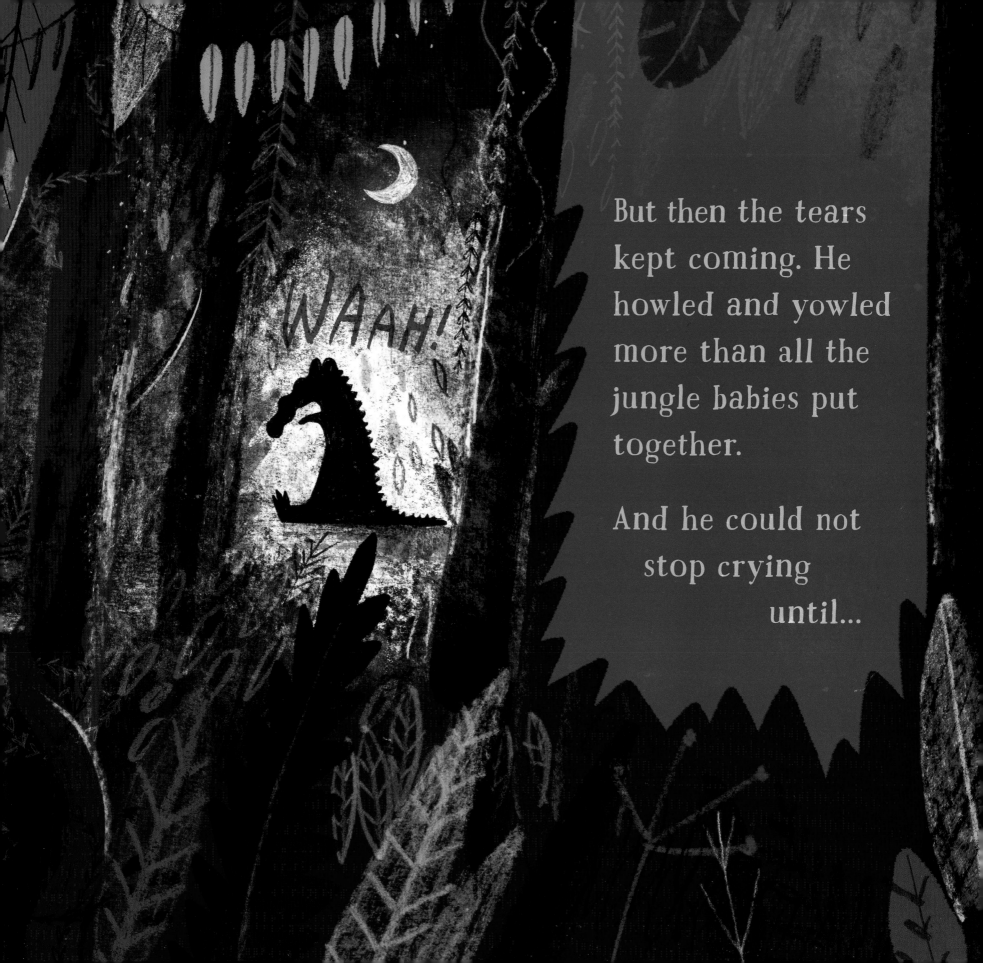

But then the tears kept coming. He howled and yowled more than all the jungle babies put together.

And he could not stop crying until...

Next morning all the animals
turned up at Alan's swamp
with his big, scary teeth.

"We'll give you back your
teeth," said Frog.

THE
RULES

"W-WEALLY?" said Alan.

"On ONE condition," said Parrot. "You have to stop scaring us."

"But what will I do? I don't know how to do ANYTHING else!"

"We have an idea," said Frog.

And so every day, after polishing his scales, sharpening his nails and brushing his big, scary teeth, Alan headed into the jungle ...

and became ... Alan, the gardener ...

WELCOME TO THE JUNGLE

GREEN FINGERS

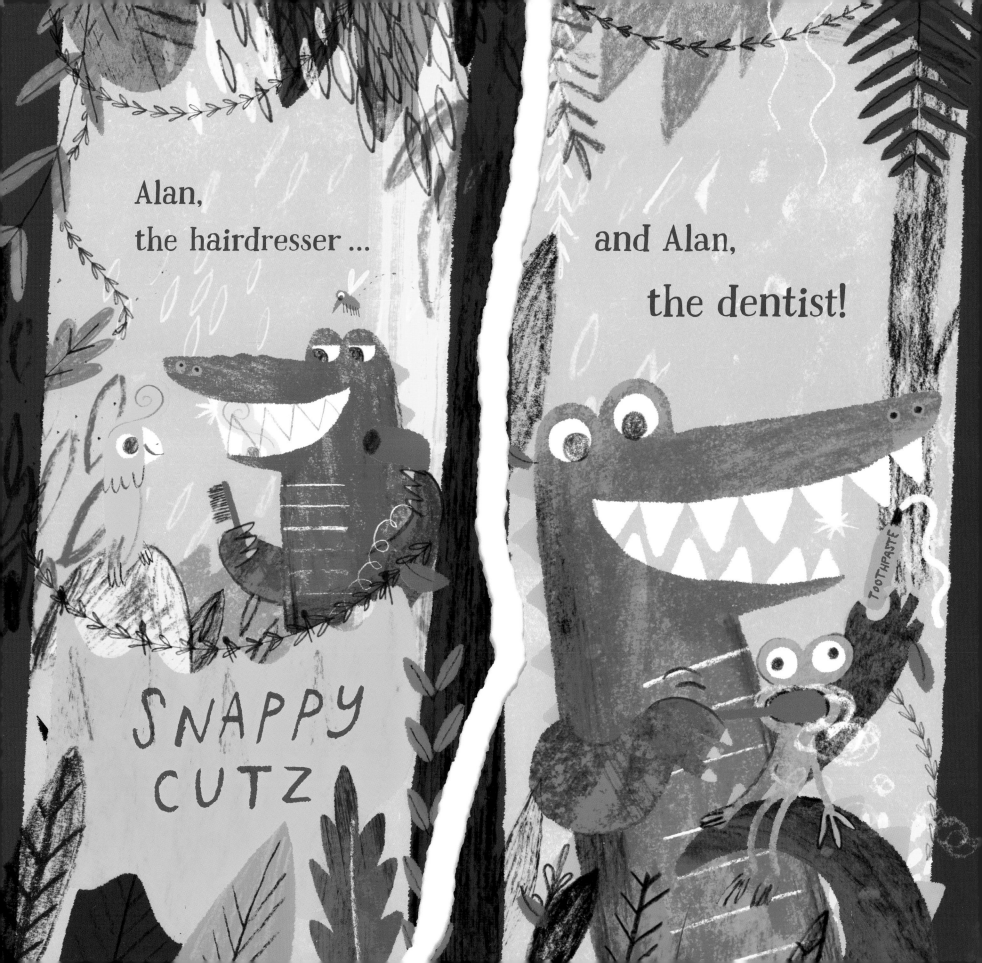

But every night ...
he became Alan the
BIG, SCARY STORYTELLER—
thrilling the jungle animals
with his terrifying tales.

"BWA-HA-HA!
I LOVE BEING SCARY,"
laughed Alan.

And sometimes...

he even let Barry borrow his teeth.